things aren't always what they seem to be

Robert H Stucky

things aren't always what they seem to be

@Copyright by Robert H Stucky, 2024

All rights reserved. This book, or any portion thereof, may not be reproduced or used in any manner whatsoever, without the express written permission of the publisher, except for brief quotations in a book review.

Printed in the United States of America.

First Printing 2024

ISBN 9798342980517

Eastcliff Editions
5908 Eastcliff Drive, Baltimore, MD 21209-3510

Cover design by Rafa León

things aren't always what they seem to be

Set primarily in a cave in an unnamed mountain somewhere in India, with his guru's explicit command to tame his mind, the protagonist goes on retreat to confront personal fears, and the shifting perception of self-identity that continually frustrates his fulfillment. A series of unexpected, surprising, and life-changing experiences radically alters both his self-understanding and world view, and redirects the protagonist's path.

things aren't always what they seem to be

Though, at first, the cave felt cold and drafty, it was reasonably spacious and was a welcome respite from the jungle heat. The ceiling was high enough for him to stand up without hitting his head on it, the floor was flat, and relatively smooth, and there appeared to be dark passages in the back that forked in opposite directions, but he had no idea where or to what they might lead. Somewhere, in the inner recesses to the left, he heard a fluttering rustle and muffled squeaks, and noticed occasional wafts of the smell of guano.

He assumed that there were probably bats roosting somewhere farther back in the cave roof.

things aren't always what they seem to be

The thought made him uneasy, as he had always found their silent flapping and erratic flittering unnerving, but he knew at least they were likely to be just small fruit bats, and not the monstrous flying foxes with the four-foot wingspans native to the region. Though scary looking, they too were fruit eaters, but, fortunately, preferred to roost in trees far down in the valley below, near banana plantations or mango groves.

He realized it was likely there were other denizens of the cave too, slithering around in the darkness— perhaps spiders, or scorpions, beetles, centipedes, or even snakes. He shuddered slightly at the thought of it. A childhood memory came to mind. He and his older brother and cousin had been sharing a basement room at his grandparents' house in Southern California, and they told him there was a tarantula in his bed. Being only five years old and not knowing what a tarantula was, he was innocent and foolish enough to ask. Thereupon, they gave him such a graphic, lurid description of the huge, bloated, hairy-legged arachnid with the eight legs and big, poisonous fangs that, to his brother's and cousin's great amusement, it sent him screaming in terror upstairs to the safety of his parents' room. He

things aren't always what they seem to be

imagined the hairy beast scuttling after him and reaching for him from every dark corner and shadow on the way. He'd had a fear of spiders ever since. And yet this was the place his master had designated for his spiritual retreat, and he was resolved to do his best to make it "home" for the duration. Apparently, facing his fears would be part of the process.

In the dim light that crept in from the entrance, he looked around and determined the best locations for him to sit, to lie down, and to eat the meager provisions he was permitted. What little food he had he stored in earthenware pots with lids, hoping to assure thereby that it was not inadvertently pilfered by any other creatures residing in the cave. Outside there was a nearby stream, and the cave had been provided with a terra cotta jug for him to draw water. He was not to leave the cave for anything other than bathing, gathering drinking water and firewood, and answering calls of nature, and even in the unlikely event another person should appear, he was to speak to no one. He was not certain that proscription included not talking to himself, but since it had not been specified, he took some

things aren't always what they seem to be

comfort in deciding it was probably ok. In fact, it was inevitable.

With a mixture of adventurous anticipation and unsettling trepidation, he lay down his backpack and began to remove its contents, arranging them in some semblance of order of accessibility that would make his stay bearable, even if not exactly comfortable. He remembered his experience on an Outward-Bound Survival trip in Maine. He was given a clear plastic tarp, a bag of trail mix, a bottle of water, and twenty feet of nylon cord, and had to create a shelter, and pass a night alone in silent reflection on Hurricane Island. The rigors of Outward Bound seemed like a stay at the Four Seasons by comparison to this far more remote and less hospitable setting.

Still, he did feel something of the satisfaction of the Sierra Club sort of modern well-equipped camper as he unloaded his knapsack. He reviewed his checklist, even though he knew he could do nothing about anything he might have forgotten to include. Fortunately, the backpack was provided with basic necessities: a flint and steel lighter, a LED solar-powered flashlight, a Swiss Army knife, a metal bowl, a water bottle,

things aren't always what they seem to be

and first aid kit. There was also an inflatable sort of yoga mat, a lightweight down sleeping bag, two changes of clothes, and a solar powered radio with a tracker chip, to be used only in an emergency. From a wilderness perspective, it almost seemed like the lap of luxury!

Somewhat reassured, he sat down at the cave entrance and looked around to get a better sense of the lay of the land. Climbing up the mountain had required too much focus to be looking around much as he went. A stream gurgled nearby, flowing from somewhere uphill to the right and down to the left, to the river in the valley below.

The mountainside was forested with a mixture of various evergreens, deodhar, and aspens, with stands of teak and mahogany and mango and banyan trees further down. The

things aren't always what they seem to be

vegetation was lush but turning brown in some places from the dry season's searing heat. The vertical patterns of ruts and exposed roots suggested that the weather was not always so sunny, and there could be torrential run-off from the mountainside during the monsoon season. For the moment, there was no rain in sight— just the suffocating humidity of its gradual approach, made all the more oppressive by the searing heat and the sluggish air flow below the tree canopy of the jungle.

Despite all that, it was quite a scenic spot. Birds rustled in the undergrowth, chirping cheerfully to each other. From somewhere further down the mountain he heard the strident cry of a peacock calling to its mate. Marmots and flying squirrels scampered busily about the rocks, munching on seeds and berries before disappearing into burrows, or climbing trees to nests somewhere out of sight. Insects buzzed. A solitary golden eagle traced languid circles in the sky, riding the air currents that gave him a spectacular vantage point from which to spot his next meal, like perusing the buffet options in a Chinese restaurant.

things aren't always what they seem to be

He inhaled deeply, as if drinking in this scenic atmosphere. "Stay in the moment!" he told himself, hoping to prevent his mind from indulging in a flood of questions to which, at the moment, at least, he had no answers.

It did strike him that to identify his sojourn in the wildness as a "spiritual *retreat*" implied running away or escaping from something. He wasn't quite sure if that indicated a certain cowardice, or the courage to face himself, undistracted and unprotected by the usual flurry of activities with which we so often avoid actually living.

He remembered one of his theology professors recounting that the so-called Desert Fathers, the first Christian monastics in the deserts of Egypt, saw their work as anything but an escape. They felt that only by emulating Jesus' living alone in the wilderness before beginning his public ministry, could they fully confront and conquer their own inner demons, undistracted by the cares of the world. They saw their retreat as actually being deployed to the front lines of the spiritual battle between good and evil.

things aren't always what they seem to be

Accordingly, his guru had insisted that he learn to tame his mind, reminding him that the definition of meditation is "the *uninterrupted* flow of awareness toward a given object", with the tantalizing proviso that that object could be internal or external, material or spiritual. Apparently, it was the clarity, intensity, and continuity of focus, not so much the content of the chosen object, that mattered most in the dynamics of self-transformation. We become what we contemplate, and anything can lead to enlightenment!

Resisting the temptation to indulge in compulsive speculation about the various things he might be inclined to run away from that made such a retreat necessary, or why he did so, he decided he should at least try to obey the guru's command to focus his attention on a single thing, and see what happened. As he sat at the mouth of the cave, his gaze fell upon a curiously shaped rock protruding from the ground in front of him. The fact that it seemed geologically distinct from other stone in the area made it more noticeable, and consequently, easier to focus upon than any others around him. So he set himself the modest challenge of looking only at that stone, and not

things aren't always what they seem to be

letting his gaze stray, or his mind become distracted by anything else. It seemed easy enough.

No sooner had he made this focal choice, however, than his ability to hold to it was challenged. All of a sudden, it was as if every bird call, every buzz of an insect, every rustle of leaves or sound of wind was demanding he shift his focus elsewhere. What had appeared to be a tranquil scene and idyllic panorama had abruptly become like staring into a turbulent pot of boiling water, obscuring the initial clarity of the mirror-like surface. It made it impossible to look at the water and see a clear reflection of his mind— or of anything else, for that matter. At least, he mused, he wouldn't fall into Narcissus' fatal trap of drowning in the beauty of his own reflection!

Rather than feeling his hoped-for tranquility, he realized he was experiencing intense agitation, and that the roiling water was, in fact, an accurate reflection of his mental state. Irresistibly, his mind was diving headfirst into a cauldron of self-recrimination, flailing in a vortex of feelings of guilt, blame, and failure.

things aren't always what they seem to be

Catching himself in the tangle of his mental agitation, and snapping out of it, he wondered impiously,

"GodDAMNIT! If I can't get my mind to shut up for even five minutes, how the FUCK am I supposed to survive this retreat?"

He felt a wave of anxiety wash over him. His gaze fell on the odd-looking stone lying innocently at the cave's entrance. It suddenly struck him as akin to the subtly camouflaged malevolent pin of a land mine, mocking him and belying a hidden danger easily triggered, a trap his mind insisted was to be carefully avoided. His initial exuberance at the quasi-romantic prospect of the adventure of a mountain retreat had quickly vanished and been replaced by a subtle sense of dread and foreboding, like a prisoner abruptly thrown into captivity with no explanation of the charges against him, or the intended length of his imprisonment.

"Ok! This is *not* gonna work!" he said to himself, trying to shake off his misgivings. "I need to get my shit together!"

things aren't always what they seem to be

He noticed that the mountain peaks across the valley were glowing with intensely golden light, and the shadows in the valley were deepening from smokey blue to an inky purple. It would be dark soon, so he set off to gather enough firewood to keep himself reasonably warm through the night, and to heat some food and drink from the meager rations with which he had been provided. He remembered the earthenware jug in the cave, and went to fill it in the stream, suddenly aware that its fragility must be carefully protected from all harm. After scrounging for firewood and kindling, as he trudged back uphill to the mouth of the cave, his arms laden with sticks and brush gleaned from the forest undergrowth, he was startled by a loud, high-pitched chirping chatter.

things aren't always what they seem to be

The sounds were emitted by a huge black cloud of bats that poured out of the cave toward him, and dispersed hungrily into the evening air, intent on gorging themselves on an abundance of insects and flowers, their sonar clicks guiding them to their prey with deadly precision and unerring efficiency.

He felt relieved, at least, that he had not been sitting in the cave when the colony of bats emerged for their evening repast. He wondered if they would return to roost with a similar synchronicity, and hoped he could avoid being there when they returned. The thought of thousands of bats flitting by him, erratically dodging to avoid bumping into him on their way in or outside, sent an involuntary shudder of fear and disgust up his spine. But just as his mind started to indulge in grim assumptions borne of the Covid-19 pandemic, elaborating on the potential horrors of bat-borne diseases, or vampiric, rabid possibilities from bat spittle or falling guano raining down on him as they passed, and his anxiety began to rise astronomically, he caught himself, and stopped.

things aren't always what they seem to be

"Thought breeds fear!" Those three words from a brilliant lecture he had heard years ago from Jiddu Krishnamurti came to him like a slap in the face, immediately snapping him out of his mental self-indulgence, and stopped his thought flow in its tracks.

As the last leather-winged stragglers emerged, he took a deep breath and mustered the courage to re-enter the cave, store his firewood, and make his campfire at the entrance, to avoid smoking himself out, and to discourage the nocturnal visit of any other creatures who might be roaming the mountainside.

As darkness fell, the symphony of Nature seemed to shift to a different movement, from

things aren't always what they seem to be

allegro to an *adagio*. The upbeat chorus of bird song died down and was reduced to the occasional distant hooting of owls in the treetops, or jungle fowl jockeying for a safe perch as they flew up into the trees to roost for the night. Other sounds seemed to issue forth now— the intermittent but disquieting bass of growls, and the sudden chilling and piercing howls of carnivores calling to each other on the prowl in the surrounding forest. These were overlaid by a steady, rhythmic chirping of insects and tree frogs, like a gentle snore that paused occasionally, as if Mother Nature was suffering from mild sleep apnea, perhaps interrupted by the ominous passing of some hungry predator looking for dinner, only to resume, once the danger had passed.

His campfire burned low as the embers seemed to tuck themselves in for the night, covering themselves with a mantel of ash. He threw on a few extra branches, banked the coals, and unrolled his mat and sleeping bag against the left wall of the cave— shaking them out first, to make sure he was not sharing them with any unwanted tenants of the biting or poisonous kind. The flames of his fire flickered and cast dramatic

things aren't always what they seem to be

shadows on the cave roof, revealing unexpected landscapes. It reminded him of when he was a small boy, lying in a meadow with his father, who challenged him to see whatever fanciful creatures he could in the shifting cloud formations scudding across the sky. Eventually, like those floating clouds, he drifted off into a somewhat fitful sleep.

His dreams were mildly unsettling, as they often had been in recent months. Ghosts from his past seemed to challenge him on the choices he had made, and his attempts at reasoning with them were met with indifference. In his dreams, he had repeatedly found himself in a church. Often the dreams were centered around rebuilding or remodeling the worship space into something more creative, more interactive, more inspiring, less superstitious, and ultimately, and more real. And there were people there who seemed eager for him to do so, but there was always either some unknown cleric or authority figure resisting and overruling the changes he sought, chastising him for doing so. The dream, no matter how recurrent, never brought any resolution, and he would always awaken with a feeling of melancholy and disappointment, mixed with relief that he was no

things aren't always what they seem to be

longer trapped in the dysfunctionality of any institutionally religious affiliation.

As he lay in that liminal state between wakefulness and sleep, pondering his fate, he suddenly had the feeling he was being watched by someone, or something, other than the ghosts of his dreams. A soft, low, guttural purring sound shook him full awake, and opening his eyes, as he looked across the smoldering remains of his campfire, he was startled to see a large black panther, lying placidly near the cave entrance. His golden eyes shone brightly as he was apparently assessing his new roommate. He yawned lazily, revealing massive canine fangs, and a bright pink tongue rough enough to rasp all the meat off the bones of any kill.

The magnificent creature showed no sign of menace, and did not appear to eye him as either a threat or a prospective meal. Still, he was certainly not expecting to share the space with a large carnivore who he knew could dispatch him to his next incarnation with one swipe of a clawed paw or a single bite of those massive canines.

things aren't always what they seem to be

Despite the proscription against talking to others, instinctively he felt an urge to communicate with this magnificent beast, reasoning that talking to an animal is not the same as talking to another person. He sat up very slowly, his back against the cave wall. The panther continued to fix his gaze on him, and though he still sensed no threat, he was cautious not to make any sudden moves that might startle it or provoke its defense mechanisms to attack him.

"Well, hello there!" he said gently. The panther blinked placidly, and his tongue licked his

things aren't always what they seem to be

chops lazily. "Aren't you beautiful?" he added, in genuine admiration.

He had a sudden, unexpected recognition of the reverence indigenous people feel for living in harmony with Nature, and seeing animals as kindred spirits. Could this beautiful creature in fact be his "spirit animal"— a companion or guide of some sort? The idea appealed to him, and as if he had understood, the panther gently laid his head on his crossed paws and seemed to doze off contentedly, like a pet dog by the fireside.

He resisted the temptation to ascribe some literary name to the beast, like the famous Bagheera of Kipling's epic story of Mowgli in the Jungle Book, but he felt a need to address the panther in some form. He thought of Kali Ma- the terrifying black goddess who vanquishes evil by scaring it to death. But his newfound den mate was decidedly male, so, however symbolically appropriate Kali's iconography, her name didn't suit him. He decided to simply call him Kala Cheetah— Hindi for Black Panther— and he wondered how such a legendary apex predator could suddenly show up in his life at this particularly prescient time and place.

things aren't always what they seem to be

He had always loved the big cats— lions, tigers, and leopards in particular. He had loved scaring his big brother by imitating their roars and growls convincingly. Their sinuous, lithe movements, their astonishing strength and speed, gave the leopards in particular an enviable grace and beauty. They had a mesmerizing strength and fluidity of supple movement, like that of a Shao-lin priest practicing kung fu. Add to that the element of those bright golden eyes, and that lustrous jet black fur, with darker spots showing up like an abalone inlay with any change of the light, and the black panther was, to him, the very embodiment of the magic and mystery of the animal kingdom.

He had read somewhere—probably in one of the National Geographics that he eagerly devoured as a kid— that unlike the lions and cheetahs of Africa, the leopards of the Indian Subcontinent, whether spotted or black, were generally nocturnal, solitary beasts who only joined others of their kind to mate. Cubs are raised in a den by the mother, but the father protects the surrounding territory, taking a more passive role, until the cubs are safely grown enough to fend for themselves. Unlike engaging in the teamwork of a pride of lions, leopards hunt stealthily alone, are masters of the sudden ambush, and can kill creatures up to ten times their size. Their powerful jaws could clamp those massive canines around their victim's neck and drag a kill a sizable distance. Endowed also with impressive, razor-sharp claws and incredibly strong legs, a leopard, disinclined to sharing a kill with anyone other than its cubs or mate, could haul the carcass up a tree trunk and hang it on a branch to keep scavengers from helping themselves to the banquet. Moreover, given the frequency with which they could be seen perched in a tree, or basking on some stone outcrop, as if thoughtfully surveying the world below, folk tradition ascribed a sort of magical wisdom, particularly to the black panther, endowing it with both lordly authority and a gift for introspection that suggested it was both the master of the jungle and the guardian of its secrets. If Kala Cheetah really was some sort of spirit guide for him, who knows what secrets he might reveal?

After reflecting on his childhood National Geographic memories and feeling comforted that he knew at least something about what to expect of leopard behavior, he finally dozed off to sleep again, feeling surprisingly safe. He slept right through the disappearance of the panther from the

things aren't always what they seem to be

cave, and later, the return of the bat colony, unaware of their satiated chittering and flapping. When he awoke, the panther was nowhere in sight. He had heard they could cover a range of many miles, marking their boundaries with scat and urine. He was uncertain as to the current whereabouts of his new-found companion, or how large a territory he prowled. For a moment he even doubted the reality of his visitor. Had he just dreamt it, or had he really been visited by a black panther? But it seemed too real and vivid to have been a figment of his imagination. It dawned on him that perhaps the other passageway at the back of the cave led to the panther's den, but he thought the better of attempting to go in there to find out.

He could hardly believe he had not yet been in this place twenty-four hours, for the previous day seemed ages ago, and had been filled with momentous events and experiences that, like the strange protruding rock at the cave's entrance, were unquestionably the tip of the iceberg of what was to come. In the plainer light of day, he eyed the rock again, as if to reassess whether it was some sort of trap, or merely a curious stone.

things aren't always what they seem to be

He recognized that stilling the mind, or eliminating all thoughts, was more than a tall order— it might actually be impossible. But then he realized his guru had not commanded he silence the mind completely, merely that he *tame* it. He remembered his guru mimicking someone with a mind out of control, as if sitting behind the steering wheel of a car careening wildly from side to side, saying with a hearty chuckle, "When the mind is not controlled, it's like trying to drive a car from the hood instead of the driver's seat. It doesn't end well!" His belly shook with laughter, and he grinned at his disciple, making it all too clear to whom he was referring. He realized that the term "master" was meant to be reflective of mastery, not ownership, and that to attain mastery over his mind was an invaluable life skill! No wonder his guru was setting him the challenge of this retreat!

He also flashed on tales his father told him of training thoroughbred horses on his grandfather's horse farm in Kentucky. "They call it 'breaking a colt'" his father explained, "but in truth, you're not breaking him, you're empowering him to run his best. First, you have to get him to accept the bit. They don't like that feeling of metal in their mouths, and fight it like hell, at first. But if

things aren't always what they seem to be

you're gentle, firm, and persistent, they get over their fear." (That seemed like a comment worth remembering for future use!) "Same thing with a saddle. Can you imagine how *you'd* feel if someone tried to strap a thirty-pound hunk of leather on your back all of a sudden? And you're not even at the point of riding yet! Getting the horse used to the weight and feel of a rider is a whole other process! If you're too gentle, the colt will never obey and learn to let you ride and control him. If you're too harsh with him, yanking on the reins, you'll hurt his mouth and break his spirit, and he'll never run a decent race. It's all about mutual understanding, communication, harmony, and balance- becoming one with your horse. But if you do it right, you help create a truly heroic beast capable of astonishing speed and strength, and of a deep loyalty, respect, and affection for its rider.

things aren't always what they seem to be

History is full of famous horses that played important roles in their riders' success — like Bucephalus, Alexander the Great's horse, or Charlemagne's Tencendur, or Zorro's horse, Tornado. Like their masters, they were noble, fearless in battle, and loyal to the end."

But his father also reminded him that if not fully tamed, or competently ridden, a horse could be skittish and easily spooked beyond even a good rider's ability to control it. (That too seemed an apt metaphor for his mind). His father, though a skilled rider, had suffered devastating damage to his knee while back home in Kentucky on college break from the polo team at Yale. He'd saddled his horse and was heading down the road with his mallet to a nearby meadow to practice his polo swing. His mount was frightened by some jalopy driving down the dirt road and back-firing— spooking his horse and causing it to bolt and ram his rider's right knee right into a nearby telephone pole. His father had to repeat his junior year in college, due to the slow and painful recovery from that injury, and suffered periodic pain in his knee for the rest of his life. He never rode again.

things aren't always what they seem to be

It seemed his guru was putting him through a similar process by limiting both his mental and physical options, to channel his potential. He could only hope his training would not include some crippling incident to drive the lesson home! He realized that like a colt that bucks and resists at first, his mind had resisted the unfamiliar discomfort of focusing on the rock at the cave entrance, looking for any excuse to avoid it. He figured learning to focus his mind was a good first step— the equivalent of learning to take the bit. Perhaps he needed to try to focus again? It would at least be a start!

In preparation, and to minimize potential distractions, he had a bite to eat, then went out to answer a call of nature, enjoying the freedom of peeing outside with such a spectacular panorama in view. He then went down to the stream to wash his face and hands before climbing back up the hill and seating himself, duly refreshed, at the cave entrance, to begin his meditation on the rock. He folded up the yoga mat to cushion his seat, and sat down on the ground, facing the curious stone.

There was a sort of vein of quartz-like milkiness swirling across the top of the rock,

things aren't always what they seem to be

almost looking like some large bird had disrespectfully left a deposit there, while flying by. But the rest of the rock was a sort of rough, nondescript, grey lump, widening at the base, as if to suggest it might be a lot bigger than it appeared. It crossed his mind that this rock might be a geode of some sort, with who knows what crystal lying within, but he was not sure he should attempt to dig it up to find out. He thought of the surprise of the archeologists who, despite having studied the massive heads of the stone figures on Easter Island for years, discovered that they were not just heads, but had entire bodies buried below them. Catching his mental tendency to indulge in endless speculation, he decided to forego the excavation option, for the time being at least, and simply try to focus all his attention on the visible portion of the rock, without interruption.

His mind did begin to wander a bit, but, he took a cue from his father's recounting how a horse trainer leads his animal by the halter, so each time his mind began to waver, he was able gently but firmly to pull its attention back to the rock lying in front of him. As he did so, he noticed that his mind was growing steadily quieter. The more he focused, the quieter it got. A deep, almost

things aren't always what they seem to be

surreal calm seemed to envelope him, and he lost all sense of time.

He had no idea how long he had remained in that altered state, but, judging from the shifting angle of sunlight and the changing direction of the tree shadows, it must have been late afternoon already.

He was shaken back into the reality of the moment by the sudden reappearance of Kala Cheetah behind him. The panther seemed to have emerged silently from the back of the cave, confirming his suspicion about the other passageway leading to his den. With the same rumbling purr that had first awakened him the day before, Kala Cheetah came up directly to him, nudging him like a pet cat begging for attention, and flopped down next to him as if waiting for a friendly scratch behind the ears, or an affectionate belly rub.

He reached out slowly and tentatively, and gently stroked the beast on the top of his head and under his chin. Kala Cheetah closed his eyes in enjoyment, rolled over on his back and nudged him to keep going, purring contentedly all the while. Lying with claws sheathed, underbelly

things aren't always what they seem to be

exposed, and paws swatting playfully in the air, his vulnerability showed his trust in his new companion. His fur was silky smooth, and he noticed that the skin of his belly was a mauve-tinged black, but his pelt actually had a leopard's jet-black spots, which were barely visible in the dark, but became more distinguishable with any movement or shift in the light. They rippled like shadows or wavelets over the surface of his muscular body, and even along the quiet switching of his long, plush tail. They made him think of the gleaming black lacquered scales of a Samurai's armor.

It would be evening soon, and time for Kala Cheetah to go out for his dinner. He knew he couldn't join the beast on the hunt, and remembered that it would soon be time for the bats to emerge from the cave too. He wondered, with a chuckle, if his new companion ever felt too hot or too lazy to hunt, and opted to swat a few bats to snack on as they emerged from the cave, like conveniently helping himself to an All You Can Eat shrimp buffet at a Red Lobster restaurant.

To his surprise, the panther yawned expansively, as if awakening from a good nap.

things aren't always what they seem to be

However, no longer purring with contentment, it was clear that cuddle time was over. With a slight growl he picked up his ears, on full alert, and suddenly leapt to his feet, his eyes glowing bright with attention, pupils narrowed in focus, and his tail twitched nervously. Then he abruptly bounded out of the cave, as if on a mission.

He wondered if the panther had got wind of some nice juicy deer or other appetizing creature nearby, and went off to feast on it. It had never occurred to him that in fact, the panther, with a sense of smell and hearing far more acute that a human's, might have picked up on the approach of some sort of intruder, and set off to investigate, to protect the cave and his companion.

The poaching of leopards had declined significantly since the end of the British Raj and the subsequent Indian restrictions placed on the fur trade, though they were still vulnerable in some regions of India, Nepal, and Bhutan, and critically endangered in Pakistan. His present location seemed far enough from any farmlands that it struck him as unlikely anyone would be trying to track down a leopard for killing livestock, much

things aren't always what they seem to be

less a villager. And given how well fed and healthy his companion clearly was, and how the surrounding jungle seemed to be teeming with more convenient food options closer to home, he doubted Kala Cheetah would have any motivation to go down to the valley and raid livestock, much less eat a villager. But there was no telling who or what might be lurking around in the forest below the cave, or why.

Sitting at the cave entrance, kindling his fire for the evening, he reconsidered the purpose of his retreat, and, looking beyond the sheer novelty of his experiences of the past two days, he began to sense a portentous shift in his own awareness to a much deeper level. That he would learn new lessons on this adventure was a given, and had already begun, but he sensed that there was much more to it than learning to live in harmony with the animal kingdom or adjusting his biorhythms to his new environment. Even his suspicion that the retreat would entail facing fears went far beyond getting over his fear of spiders, or the flitting of bats. It struck him as more than surprising that encountering a full-grown black panther in his prime "up close and personal", though unexpected, had not provoked in him any fear at

things aren't always what they seem to be

all. On the contrary. The two of them seem to have bonded immediately. He couldn't help but wonder why and how that was even possible.

He resisted the temptation to interpret the significance of Kala Cheeta through a mythological or theological filter. He could not think of the iconography of any Hindu or Buddhist deity whose mount was a black panther, in any case, so it seemed a moot point. If Kala Cheetah did have some specifically spiritual significance or meaning, he had no idea what it was, or why. It seemed a major part of his retreat was going to be learning how to suspend his judgment, face things head on, and not project any particular expectations onto the situation of the moment.

He had heard stories and legends of wild animals becoming tame in the presence of a holy being: like the birds listening to the preaching of St. Anthony, or the Wolf of Gubbio bowing in submission to St. Francis, or Siddhartha Gautama in meditation being shielded from the monsoon rain by the hood of a huge cobra. He even recalled the story told by an elderly disciple of his guru's guru, whose ashram was surrounded by thick forest.

things aren't always what they seem to be

One night, unable to sleep, the devotee awoke to the light of a full moon and saw the master walking out alone into the jungle. Consumed with curiosity, he got up quietly and followed. The master, wearing nothing but a lungoti— a loincloth— walked at an unexpectedly brisk pace, despite his severely arthritic knees, and was soon out of sight. But the devotee continued down the trail set by the master until he came upon a clearing. There, on a bed of tall grass, sat his guru. To his amazement, he was talking softly to a full-grown Bengal tiger, who, like Kala Cheetah, sprawled out at his side, purring with contentment while the master stroked his head lovingly.

He certainly didn't see any connection between himself and those saintly beings, but he couldn't help wondering what their own self-experience had been in those moments that the hagiographers have so gilded and enhanced? He did recognize that there seemed to be at least a pattern of their interacting with nature in ways that appeared to be far more intimate and less confrontational than most people's. Given his present experiences, the human presumption of

things aren't always what they seem to be

innate entitlement to dominate nature for personal convenience now seemed utterly unfounded.

Presumably, each of those saints had learned to tame his mind, and thereby render himself vibrationally un-threatening and correspondingly more receptive to wild animals, and their mutual well-being. Consequently, the animals had responded in kind. A week ago, he would have been highly agitated at even the thought of inhabiting a cave in which a huge colony of bats perched during the day. Still less would he have been open to the possibility of sharing a den with a full-grown black panther, completely unarmed and unprotected. And yet, contrary to his own expectations, he had adapted to both almost instantly, to the point that a day later, whether winged or clawed, his neighbors seemed totally normal to him. This shift in perspective clearly seemed to have some sort of proportional correlation to his level of mental agitation— or lack thereof. Maybe the exercises of focusing on the rock were more productive than he had realized.

He decided to try to sit for a more prolonged period of focusing on it this time.

things aren't always what they seem to be

Though geologically unremarkable in appearance, the unexpected calming of his mind by focusing on the rock seemed to endow it with a new-found, almost radiant, mystical significance. He wondered if it would be any different focusing on it in the evening, instead of in broad daylight. After all, with his fire near the cave entrance, there was at least enough light for him to see the rock clearly outside. Maybe that way he'd be less prone to distractions?

Aside from the general challenges of hygiene in a cave on a mountaintop in a jungle, he realized that the Hindu and Muslim customs of ablutions before prayer or worship made an intrinsic sort of sense. They were a way of "cleaning the slate" and redirecting attention from mundane matters to the inner task at hand. So, deciding to make it part of his own practice, too, after building his fire for the evening and eating his Spartan fare, he went out to take a piss and wash his face, hands, and feet before returning to meditate on the mysterious rock.

Suddenly, he heard a rustling in the brush. Instinctively on alert, he backed his way carefully up the hill to the protection of the cave. His fear

things aren't always what they seem to be

mounting, his eyes searched through the steadily dimming light of dusk for any possible threat, or any predator on the prowl.

To his relief, Kala Cheetah emerged from the underbrush and headed straight for the mouth of the cave at a determined trot, just as the bat colony began to deploy its forces into the evening air. As if waiting for the changing of the guard, the panther stood aside as the bats fluttered out, and only when they all seemed to have exited the cave did he and his human companion enter. They sat down by the fire, and Kala Cheetah sniffed him, as if to learn if he'd been hanging out with anyone else in his absence.

"Hey there buddy! What have you been up to?" he asked, as he stroked the panther on the top

things aren't always what they seem to be

of his head, seriously curious as to what had provoked his sudden departure, and what he had encountered out there. Needless to say, there was no articulate response from the beast, but his purring and gentle nudging seemed to indicate that all was well, for the moment at least. He felt reassured that the panther did not seem inclined to go back out to hunt and was content to lie protectively dozing by the fire.

In the oddly domestic security of their companionship, he decided to proceed with his meditation on the rock and settled himself on his folded mat at the mouth of the cave, his back to the warmth of the fire. With the fire behind him, he cast a shadow on the top of the rock, rendering it barely visible in the gathering dark of night. Still, he kept his attention at the spot where the milky whiteness seemed to erupt, and to his amazement, the top of the rock started to glow in the dark.

things aren't always what they seem to be

Looking up, he discovered that the full moon was rising over the mountains on the other side of the valley, and a single beam of ivory white moonlight had threaded its way between the tree branches to fall directly on the top of the rock. The quartz-like whiteness at its top suddenly seemed to become radiant, and dazzlingly alive, like a gardenia flower opening.

From somewhere in the vegetation nearby, the intoxicating smell of *raat-ki-rani*—the night blooming jasmine the Indians called Queen of the Night — unexpectedly filled the air. Its signature perfume is so all-enveloping that it is famously impossible, by smell alone, to pin down from

things aren't always what they seem to be

where it is emanating. The combination of the glowing moonlight and the heavenly fragrance surrounding him was utterly entrancing, and he found himself drawn into a depth of inner quiet he had never experienced before. Not a ripple of thought stirred the surface of his mind. Time seemed to stand still.

"Well, THAT's a step in the right direction!" he heard the voice of his guru say, with a tinge of bemused sarcasm, but with crystal clarity. It was so startlingly loud and clear that he actually spun around to see if his guru had somehow appeared by the fireside. Kala Cheetah lay watching him attentively, still purring softly. He had the uncanny feeling that the panther's purring was weaving some sort of spell, as if to open him to new modes of communication. He shook himself to snap out of what he assumed must be some sort of fantasy.

"Pull yourself together! You're supposed to *tame* your mind, not indulge it!" he told himself. The magic of the moment having passed, the moonlight shifted, dappling the forest floor with lacey shadows. No longer glowing on the top of the rock, in the darkness the stone became once again, ordinary and unremarkable. Suddenly

things aren't always what they seem to be

overcome with sleep, he said, "I think that's about enough for one night!", as much to himself as to his furry companion. He banked the fire and crawled into his sleeping bag, and promptly drifted off while Kala Cheetah patiently gave him an oddly penetrating sort of look, as if seeing right into him somehow.

As he slept, he began to dream. In his dream he was sitting facing Kala Cheetah, who sat looking at him intently, almost expectantly, as if waiting for his companion to finally realize something important. His look had the persistence of a pet cat demanding to be fed, and not about to give up until he got the desired response. The panther even uttered the big cat equivalent of a sort of pleading meow to underscore the importance of paying attention to him. As he stared back, wondering what was going on in the beast's mind to account for such a penetrating look, he gasped in astonishment, for the figure of Kala Cheetah was suddenly morphing into the form of his guru! The master sat cross-legged, grinning at him by the fire, his mirthful eyes twinkling with bemused enjoyment. His mind was momentarily stunned into silence, and then immediately flooded with questions. Was he

things aren't always what they seem to be

hallucinating? What was really going on here? Where the hell did the panther go?

"Baba?" He said incredulously, with a mixture of worry and relief, still looking around the cave for signs of the panther. Finding none, his gaze returned, inquisitively, to the face of his master, who seemed to be waiting for his full attention before speaking.

He raised his right hand, half waving in greeting, half in a mudra of blessing. "*Bahut achcha, bahut achcha*" (Very good, very good) the guru muttered, almost as if talking to himself. He knew from experience that interpreting the guru's words could be a tricky business, for they generally held multi-layered meaning, and usually only the first was obvious, though often of only secondary importance. Did his "Very Good" mean he was making good spiritual progress on this retreat? Or that the master was pleased with the student? Or perhaps was it an approval of his student's utter bewilderment, as if his stupor was the necessary precondition for the next step in this retreat process? Perhaps it was all three?

Somehow hoping or expecting the guru to provide more explicit instruction, or some clear

things aren't always what they seem to be

indication of what he was to do next, he was a bit disappointed not to hear any response. A soft noise seemed to break his REM cycle, and opening his eyes, he saw Kala Cheetah, still sitting calmy staring at him. His guru, however, seemed to have disappeared. His mind was not yet ready to entertain the possibility that the stories he had heard of indigenous shamans in the Americas, or even yogis in the Himalayas, were "shape-shifters," capable of changing their appearance into that of some animal, were not mere fantasy or folklore.

Without further ado, noting the human's confusion and resistance to embracing a new dimension of reality, the panther slowly stood up, stretched luxuriously, blinked amiably, and turned, silently disappearing into the darkness as he walked back into the tunnel leading to his den.

"Kala Cheetah! Wait!" he cried instinctively, suddenly pained by the possibility of being all alone to face whatever was going on. The panther stopped for a moment, looking back over his shoulder at his ward. His purring almost sounded like the sotto voce murmur of *mantra japa*. Snuffing softly, Kala Cheetah then continued

things aren't always what they seem to be

on into the comfortable darkness of the inner recesses of his den, almost as if inviting his companion to follow him inside.

His reason desperate to exercise some sort of control over this reality-challenging sequence of events, he quickly grabbed his LED flashlight and his Swiss Army knife, opening it to the largest blade, as if to arm himself against unseen dangers. The absurdity of thinking a four-inch Swiss Army knife blade could be an effective defense against any and all attackers, was beside the point. Clutching the knife in one hand, with the other he switched on his flashlight, its bright beam slicing a

things aren't always what they seem to be

blinding white swathe through the darkness of the tunnel leading to Kala Cheetah's inner sanctum, and he tentatively crept down the passageway.

The tunnel turned to the right and suddenly widened into a sizable chamber with no visible means of egress other than way he came in. Yet Kala Cheetah was nowhere to be seen! Once again, heart pounding, his mind was triggered into a fear response, desperate to locate his four-footed companion, or at least rationally explain his disappearance. Had his whole saga with Kala Cheetah been a figment of his imagination? And what about the brief appearance of his guru, in such convincing and vivid detail? Was all this

things aren't always what they seem to be

some sort of dream or hallucination? Was he delusional? He felt goose bumps all over his body.

"Face your fear! Face your fear!" he told himself. "What is it that you're afraid of?" He sat down in the middle of the chamber and scanned the entire periphery with his flashlight. To his surprise, there was nothing particularly noteworthy to be seen, much less anything clearly sinister or frightening, other than the disquieting disappearance of Kala Cheetah. It was an empty space.

"What the….f? " He sat bewildered, and uneasy. Realizing he had been hyperventilating in panic, he forced himself to breathe more slowly and deeply, and gradually his fear began to subside. Eventually, his mind grew quiet, and he sat to ponder his fate. Still perplexed by the disappearance of Kala Cheetah, and wary of wasting the flashlight battery and ending up trapped in the dark, he got up and slowly headed back to the mouth of the cave and the possibility of recharging the battery in the sunlight.

He noticed with mild surprise that the improbable novelty of the panther's presence seemed more real to him than the familiar

things aren't always what they seem to be

appearance of his beloved guru. Consequently, Kala Cheetah's sudden unexplained disappearance was strangely more unsettling than that of his guru—presumably because the apparition of mystical visions of saints and sages was a more "normal" part of his belief system than the possibility of living peaceably with a widely feared apex predator. There was simply no precedent for that in his life experience.

He did stop to consider, however, what he heard his guru say to him when his mind became so calm: "Well, THAT's a step in the right direction!" Could the disappearance of the panther be symbolic of the cessation of thought— the step in the right direction toward taming his mind? What did the panther embody, for him? Was it good, or evil? Was he the Shadow incarnate? If Kala Cheetah really was his "spirit animal" or guide, where was he leading him? To an empty cave? Did its emptiness mean something?

His initial reaction to the vanishing panther was NOT mental silence, to say the least— quite the contrary— but after he sat breathing, and scanned the cave to find it totally empty, his mind

things aren't always what they seem to be

did, in fact, calm down. It struck him that the guru's stipulation that he not leave the cave except for water, firewood, and calls of nature, left him with no place to go. Nowhere, except of course, within! Apparently, he was being directed to go beyond the surface chatter of his mind to inner depths that remained, as yet, unexplored.

Even though he grasped the need to face his fears, surprisingly, when he asked himself overtly, "What are you afraid of?", there was no response. Nothing in particular came up for him. He couldn't tell if this was just his mental habit of avoidance, instinctively evading the discomfort of whatever darker elements lay hidden below, just waiting to ambush him. But the visceral panic that had overcome him in Kala Cheetah's empty den made it clear that fear had not yet been fully vanquished, and that it was often irrational. Apparently, it remained alive and well deep within him, lying in wait, and ever ready to rush to the surface of his awareness and ambush him in a heartbeat, randomly triggered by God only knows what thought, memory, or experience.

He was reminded of watching horror movies— especially those that portrayed the

things aren't always what they seem to be

ghosts of people who had died cruelly or violently— and how the sudden appearance of a blurry apparition, or the haunting sound of faint music, or footsteps, or the sudden squeaky opening or closing of a door, could trigger a visceral response in him, making literally every single hair stand up on end, and sending the shudder of an electric chill surge through his body.

He knew, of course, that the filmmaker was deliberately playing with the audience, counting on the ability to trigger a fear response as a necessary component of the unfolding storyline. He knew a bunch of adrenaline junkies who loved horror movies for that very rush of fear— the emotional equivalent of the sudden precipitous drop of a roller coaster— but it was never an experience he relished. He preferred to avoid such films— and roller coasters— altogether.

His wife and son enjoyed crime dramas— the grimmer the better— but he had little stomach for the exceptionally cruel or perverse. Even his love for historical dramas balked at times, not because of the swashbuckling brutality of medieval carnage. It was the vitriol and emotional cruelty, to say nothing of the loathsome hypocrisy

things aren't always what they seem to be

of religious zealots' attacks on those whose beliefs differed from their own, that, in addition to fear, always triggered the most intense mixture of anger, outrage, and immense sorrow in him.

But that fear of psychological cruelty was not just limited to a cinematic response. He had vivid real-life memories too. He flashed on visiting an 18th century plantation outside of Charlestown in West Virginia, years ago. The property had been bought by a group of friends intent on creating a sort of Hippie commune, and refurbishing the stately mansion to create a retreat center there. He knew the original owners had been slaveholders and presumed that their prosperity had been at the expense of generations of people they abusively considered no more than property for them to use at their pleasure. Having wrestled with his own family's complicity in that dark period of American history, and hoping to atone for it, he had become an ardent supporter of civil rights and felt increasing discomfort when visiting the historical landmarks that revealed how much American history had been glossed over by the "ruling class" of affluent white folks, whose success was built on the backs of enslaved people.

things aren't always what they seem to be

As he toured the once grand plantation house, he began to experience a visceral sadness, which became overwhelming as he went down a servants' back stairway to the mansion's kitchen on the lower level. The sense of inescapable suffering and miserable oppression became so intense, he could hardly breathe, and had to excuse himself from the tour to go outside for air. The kitchen and stairway, in particular, felt oddly cold, despite the heat of summer. He hadn't actually *seen* the ghosts of the plantation's slaves, but he had felt their chilling presence and their helpless agony there as vividly as if they had been standing right in front of him. The weight of that

things aren't always what they seem to be

sorrow remained with him for days after returning home from the commune.

Since that time, he had often been deeply affected by the feel of a place— whether positive or negative— and had realized that history was not just the record of buildings and human creativity, but was the chronicle and imprint of the full range of experiences undergone by the people who had created and inhabited them. Knowing how often the greatest structures of human engineering were accomplished by force of the whip and the oppression of slaves and captives involuntarily pressed into the ruler's service, he began to understand how an empath could feel overwhelmed by the vibe of their suffering. Likewise, he came to a new appreciation of the underlying pathos of how the beauty, grandeur, and opulence of human creativity could simultaneously be a celebration of our highest attributes, and an attempt to hide or compensate for the depravity that, too often, the patrons of such achievements sought to conceal from others, and even from themselves. His observation reconfirmed the pithy sarcasm of his favorite bumper sticker: *Denial is not a River in Egypt.*

things aren't always what they seem to be

But all that seemed a bit academic and theoretical compared to the situation at hand. He suddenly wondered if, by quieting the mind sufficiently to enter into a sort of trance-like state, he might be able to discover and reveal his own elusive fears, and whatever was likely to trigger them. Was there someone, some place or something that truly terrified him that he was avoiding? Were there actual memories of his own misdeeds or suffering in past lives waiting to ambush him with guilt, and overpower him with remorse? And if so, what were they, and why could he not recall them?

He remembered reading of the work of the Swiss psychologist, Carl Jung, a disciple of Sigmund Freud, who sought to explore the human psyche from a more spiritual perspective. Jung spoke of the Shadow— the dark side of human nature— as something innately within all of us. He was convinced that the unavoidable challenge of spiritual growth and psychological health was to first accept and embrace that darkness, in order to vanquish and harness it, to achieve real inner harmony.

things aren't always what they seem to be

He also spoke of the *anima* and *animus*— the feminine and masculine principles whose interaction provided psychological balance. This was not a new idea. The Ancient World had taught as much for millennia. The Tantrics spoke of the balance between Shiva and Shakti. The Taoists referred to the same challenge in terms of Yin and Yang. The shamans of Mexico spoke of the Tonal and Nagual. All of them saw that the constant interplay of polarities, both physically and metaphysically, whatever their cultural context or nomenclature, is clearly intrinsic to all activity. Simply selectively preferring the positive, or obsessing about the negative, as if its counterpart could be ignored, is not a viable option.

So, it seemed it was time to try more deliberately to discover what was lurking in the shadows of his own psyche. Was there something out of balance, and if so, what was it? With no Google or Internet to draw on for research, and no edifying reading material at hand, his only option was the time-honored ancient practice the yogis and sages called *atma vicara*— self-inquiry. But the problem with asking himself what he was afraid of seemed to be his stubborn resistance and unwillingness to actually listen for or accept the

things aren't always what they seem to be

answer. He would apparently have to trick his mind into surrendering control, if he was going to learn anything useful.

"I guess it's time to visit the rock again!" he told himself. This time, rather than simply sitting passively staring at the stone, he decided that if he was to dig any deeper psychologically, perhaps he should do a little physical digging too. Using his Swiss Army knife, he began to scratch around the base of the rock, removing surrounding dirt to try to see more of the stone itself. As he had suspected, the rock proved to be much bigger than it looked, and the swirling white seen at the top turned out to be a vein that ran down the far side of the stone. There was a good chance it was some sort of quartz geode. As he scratched and clawed and scraped away, trying to dislodge the rock and examine it more fully, it suddenly cracked and split open to reveal a large and dazzling cluster of clear, deep purple amethyst crystals.

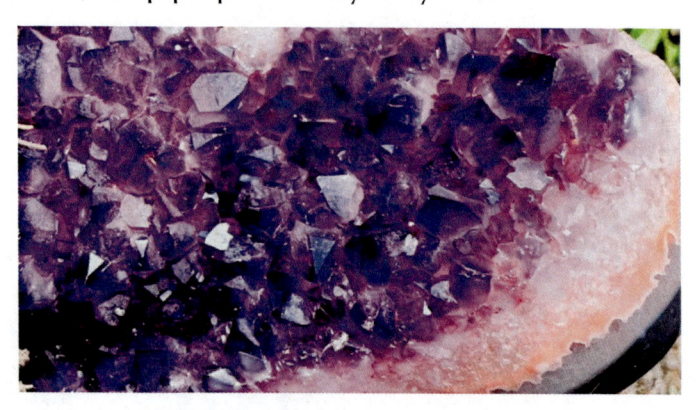

things aren't always what they seem to be

Not being prone to millennial assertions of the benefits of crystal gazing, nevertheless, despite his skepticism, he had heard that amethyst was purported to have great spiritual powers— particularly of healing and protection, mental peace, clarity, wisdom, and compassion. That seemed appropriate, or at least hopeful, under the circumstances. The beauty of the crystals was, in fact, captivating. Indian culture took such matters very seriously. Even Roman Catholicism had often resorted to using amethyst for the rings and pectoral crosses of prelates. Perhaps they did so because one of its properties was to protect against drunkenness, which was an occupational hazard for those regularly charged with the ritual transubstantiation of fortified wine they sacramentally consumed as the Blood of Christ! So, he deduced that this massive geode of gem quality crystals would presumably have such curative and protective powers in abundance.

"Well, that's helpful!" he thought. "If I'm supposed to face my dark side, at least there's some comfort in having this nuclear arsenal at the ready, just in case, even if I have no clue as to how to make use of it!" Leaving the geode open, like an oyster displaying its pearls, he went through his

things aren't always what they seem to be

preparatory ablutions, and then sat down at the cave entrance to contemplate the stone. Released from the darkness of lying hidden underground for eons, shards of sunshine reflected off the crystals, showering him with their virginal purple light. It reminded him of the inspiring experience of feeling cleansed by the holy light of the stained glass of the Sainte Chapelle in Paris on a sunny day. "No wonder laser therapy has become such a thing!" he mused.

His mental activity and breathing steadily slowed as he basked in that purple light, until it finally became as calm and ripple-free as a mountain lake. Content to settle into reveling in that peace and quietude, he was in no way prepared for what was about to happen. Suddenly his breathing became rapid, shallow and agitated, and the glassy calm of his mental state began to move ominously. It was as if some great ravenous beast had been aroused and was thrashing upward to attack him from somewhere deep below the surface, and, fast approaching, was now just out of sight. Though, as yet unseen, the immanent menace was intensely terrifying, all the more so since he had no clue as to the nature of the threat, or what had troubled the waters of his mind.

things aren't always what they seem to be

Just before the mysterious peril broke the surface to reveal itself, he heard the angry, ferocious roar of a leopard, and spun around to see Kala Cheetah leap right over him and land, four footed, crouching, fangs bared in fierce grimace, ears pinned back, fur bristling, claws unsheathed, and tail twitching menacingly. He stood there, right in front of the rock, snarling and hissing as if to ward off the attack of this unknown and unseen threat.

As he took in this unexpected sight, uncertain whether the unseen threat or the panther

things aren't always what they seem to be

was more terrifying, the underwater thrashing ceased immediately, and the surface of his mind gradually became calm, once again. With barely a ripple, like the swish of a leviathan's tail, as it returned to the deep, it left only a sort of unanswered vestigial swirl of disquietude, wondering what the *hell* that was all about, and the worry that it might erupt again at some unguarded moment, when his protection was uncertain.

Then a rush of relief swept over him—partly for having avoided a close encounter of the monstrous kind, and partly for the consolation of the welcome return of his feline den mate and apparent guardian. Gradually the pounding of his heart returned to its normal rhythm.

"*Shanta raho. Sub kuchch thik hain!* Be at peace, everything is alright". His guru's reassuring voice was clearly audible, but looking around, the master was nowhere in sight. The words, in fact, seemed to have been uttered by Kala Cheetah himself! As he stared in disbelief at the panther, the big cat nodded, as if to say, "That's right! You did hear those words come from me! Don't look so surprised! Things are often not what they seem

things aren't always what they seem to be

to be." Then he added, somewhat cryptically, "The guru's shakti can assume any form at will, and is ever at the master's service. It is the master's job and binding commitment to guide and protect his disciple on his path to realization. Remember, all existence is simply a manifestation of Chiti Shakti— the singular, divine power of Consciousness— and your sole purpose in this life is to become anchored in that realization."

It struck him that this experience was not like some AI simulation, or Disney style animation of a talking panther with an appropriately upbeat, catchy music soundtrack. The voice was real, but was not formed by any discernibly coordinated movement of lips, or mouth, or tongue. It was more like a telepathic transmission directly from one mind to another. As if in confirmation, the panther drew nearer and gently nudged his forehead, holding his head still, forehead to forehead, for a moment, like the reverent tete à tete of two Tibetan monks greeting each other in a meeting of the mindful. Yet there was nothing about it that felt artificial or contrived.

However, even the Guru's comforting assurance that "everything is alright" did not fully

things aren't always what they seem to be

assuage his anxiety. It reminded him of an experience years earlier. He had been charged with the care of a beautiful pair of Australian black swans given to the ashram. Sweet tempered and friendly, he named them after the divine couple, Radha and Krishna, and would call to them at feeding time. They would call back to him, serenely floating across the lake, and come eat out of his hand. One day he noticed that Krishna seemed uncomfortable, as if in pain, and he didn't want to eat. He told his guru he was taking the beautiful bird to the veterinarian. Baba had said, "Everything will be alright."

things aren't always what they seem to be

The bird proved to be suffering from incurable lead poisoning, having inadvertently gobbled up some lead shot from the lake bottom, presumably from hunters. Sadly, Krishna died. That did not seem "alright" to him, until he heard the guru say that any creature or person with the good fortune to leave their body in the abode of a saint was guaranteed a blessed life in their next incarnation. Apparently, to accurately assess whether something was alright required a longer view than he was used to having and might run quite counter to his own expectations and assumptions!

So now, even on the assumption that everything really was alright, he realized he needed to take fuller stock of his situation, and assess just exactly what "everything" meant, realizing that his definition of that word and the guru's definition might not be the same. Baba's words resounded in his brain like the polyphonic hum of a Tibetan singing bowl: "All existence is simply a manifestation of Chiti Shakti— the singular, divine power of Consciousness— and your sole purpose in life is to become anchored in this realization."

things aren't always what they seem to be

"O.k., fine!" he said to himself, a bit annoyed at what felt like the guru's deliberate vagueness of instruction. He asked, half-out loud, "But how, exactly, am I supposed to do that?"

He had to admit that in those moments when his mind was calm, his experience always changed for the better. The relief of being able to step away from his constantly churning thought patterns was palpable and immediate, but the effort of maintaining the focus required to enter that thought-free state and remain there for any length of time could be exhausting. It somehow seemed more difficult than being a simple matter of choice. He felt like he needed to be able to *do* something to maintain that focus— some specific practice to deprogram his overthinking mind, and create an alternative habit, or way of being. But he had no clue what that practice could be.

things aren't always what they seem to be

He stood at the entrance of the cave, looking out over the jungle landscape and the open geode at his feet. Shoving his hands in his pockets in frustration, he suddenly felt in his right hand the *japa mala* his guru had given him years ago. Not being particularly inclined to religious rituals, and somewhat put off by those who seemed obsessively devout and immersed in such things, he had kept the rosary in his pocket for its sentimental value as a gift from the master, like a sort of good luck charm, but had never seriously tried to make use of it. Truth be told, he had never even really considered it as a useful tool. It was just a keepsake from his teacher— what culturally

things aren't always what they seem to be

ignorant Westerners dismissively trivialized as "worry beads". He felt surprisingly embarrassed that he had never taken seriously the Indians' insistence that every action and word of the guru can be full of meaning and instruction. That kind of credulous devotion seemed like sentimental exaggeration to him— like the besotted enthusiasm of new-found romance— until now.

He suddenly remembered a dream of a statue of his guru sitting on an altar, draped in radiant silk, and holding a japa mala of large amethyst beads! Now, the clear crystal beads of his own mala seemed to be calling him insistently to continuously repeat the mantra his guru had given him, as an actual vehicle and transmitter of the guru's own power and realization.

things aren't always what they seem to be

Once again, he sat down in the entrance to the cave. Pulling the mala from his pocket the beads clicked softly, and the gold tassel gleamed brightly in the sunshine. He began to pronounce the mantra out loud, repeating it with each bead as it passed through his fingertips — *Guru Om, Guru Om, Guru Om…* Gradually it seemed to take on a natural rhythm of its own, like the rhythm of his breathing. The resonance echoed off the vaulted ceiling of the cave, magnifying his voice and surrounding him with the sound of it. It had the acoustic effect of an entire chorus chanting, and at the same time, created a sort of low, continuous purr, like the sound made by Kala Cheetah, that had an almost hypnotic, spell-binding vibratory effect.

He remembered Baba explaining that the guru is not a person, but rather, a cosmic principle— the transformative, grace-bestowing power of Divine Consciousness. The syllable Gu represents darkness and ignorance, and Ru represents the dispelling of that darkness by the light of realization. Om is like the Big Bang— the primordial sound from which Creation sprang, which continues to reverberate throughout all existence, and to which everything will ultimately

things aren't always what they seem to be

return. So, *Guru Om* means that that Primordial Source is what removes the darkness of our ignorance, and bestows the omnipresent grace of enlightenment on us— the lasting experience of our own eternal interconnectedness with all Creation.

As he pondered this meaning, wondering how to shed light on whatever darkness lurked inside him that might need to be removed, for him to be able to experience that interconnectedness continuously, he found himself being pulled deeper and deeper within. Gradually, he lost all sense of bodily existence or separate identity— there was only pure, non-judgmental awareness. His breathing slowed, and the beads of his japa mala seemed suddenly heavier, as if the telling of them was more work than he could stand. He stopped chanting out loud and began to simply repeat the mantra to himself mentally, in silence, his fingers barely able to keep moving the beads, until finally both his mantra repetition and the movement of his rosary through his fingers stopped altogether, and he felt pulled inward to an even deeper space, devoid of all image and form. It was as velvety black as Kala Cheetah himself, and yet strangely luminous at the same time.

things aren't always what they seem to be

As he sat there in deep meditation, his body began to tremble. He had the bizarre sensation of observing himself with utter clarity and complete detachment, and at the same time felt a raging visceral force surging upward within him, until it burst forth in a deafening roar, like that of Kala Cheetah leaping to protect him. His roar even seemed to disconcert the bat colony deep within the cave, who chittered for a few moments in startled response, before settling back down to roost. But this time, the roar was coming from him, not from anyone or anything external to him! Kala Cheetah was nowhere in sight. Nor was his guru. He had the vivid sensation that his own forearms were covered with black fur, his hands had become paws, his fingers sported long, sharp claws, and, spontaneously, he began to claw the ground in front of where he sat, snarling ferociously all the while. The urge to roar continued, and he felt the rage of a caged animal wanting to lash out at unseen captors.

He had been totally unprepared for his experience of seeing Kala Cheetah morph into the form of his guru, and then later hearing his guru's voice coming from Kala Cheetah. But he had not seriously pondered the legends of shape-shifting

things aren't always what they seem to be

spirit guides, and had sort of dismissed that odd possibility as simply a visionary phenomenon, intrinsic to the lore of the yogic practices in which he was now engaged. He had felt no need to decipher it. But this experience of feeling *himself* to *be* Kala Cheetah, with a personal but unremembered history of having been previously captured and caged, but now freed, was truly staggering. Even more so because it led him inevitably to recognize that if Kala Cheetah and Baba were one and the same, different manifestations of the same consciousness, then he too implicitly shared in that oneness!

The guru had said as much many times, but it had always seemed theoretical and philosophical to him. Now there was a literal, experiential reality to it that shook him profoundly, and both inspired and terrified him. He had no idea what to *do* with that perception, or how to distinguish between having a psychotic episode and a spiritual breakthrough. Yet all this occurred to him as a calm witness of the events and sensations, with a willingness to simply let them play out, without any need to identify with them, nor to make any deliberate attempt to intervene, direct, avoid, or control them.

things aren't always what they seem to be

His roaring gradually subsided, as did his enraged, involuntary clawing of the ground, leaving only the testimony of deep grooves in the dusty floor of the cave as a confirmation of the event. Once again, he had the experience of returning to a state of deep calm, almost as if some emotional toxin had just been flushed out of his system, leaving him feeling lighter and more energetic, but without any urgency to *do* anything in particular. Other than eat!

He realized he was suddenly ravenously hungry, but that his provisions were steadily diminishing. He particularly craved something sweet but had nothing in his supplies that seemed likely to satisfy that yearning. He remembered Baba saying that deep meditation releases a lot of energy and can generate a lot of inner heat, and that the best way to handle that was to eat something sweet, drink water, and smell flowers, or perfume. He certainly was feeling the inner heat, but saw no flowers in bloom nearby, and had no candy or sweets stored in his terra cotta pots. He stepped out of the cave to go fill his water jug, thinking that if he drank at least, it might cool him down a bit, fill his stomach some, and deflect his craving.

things aren't always what they seem to be

He was reminded of Baba telling him that the Shakti was all-knowing and would provide whatever he needed. That too had seemed fanciful and naïve to him— sort of "magical thinking"— but as he stood at the mouth of the cave, he heard a loud buzzing. Looking up at the crags above the entrance, he was surprised to see a huge beehive. He had not noticed it before. Globs of honey were literally dripping from the honeycomb and slowly trickling downward toward the cave entrance. He suddenly recalled a line from the Bible about God providing nourishment for His faithful with "honey from the rock"!

things aren't always what they seem to be

Wary of the danger of stirring up the hive and being badly stung with no medical treatment available for miles around, he grabbed a smoking branch from his fire, hoping the smoke would provide enough of a sedative to the bees to permit him to gather at least a piece of honeycomb without being attacked. Wild jungle bees were reputed to have a particularly painful sting.

Carefully and slowly, he managed to climb up the rock face to the lowest point where he could see any accumulation of honey. As luck would have it, it appeared that a chunk of honeycomb had broken off from the bottom of the hive, and was now sitting perched precariously on a sort of ledge-like protrusion of the rock face. Holding the still smoking branch, he reached up with it and took a swipe at the chunk of honeycomb, grazing it slightly, but not enough to knock it to the ground below.

"Focus! Focus!" he told himself, and reaching as far up as he dared, forcing himself to overcome his vertigo, and on the verge of falling, he swung the smoking branch again. This time the branch seemed to hit the honeycomb right between the wax and the ledge upon which it

things aren't always what they seem to be

balanced. Whether from the force of the blow, or perhaps the heat of the smoldering branch softening the wax, he saw a number of bees flee, and fly up toward the main hive, just as the honey-laden comb slipped and finally fell to the ground in front of the cave entrance.

Feeling a mixture of awe and elation at this serendipitous and providential bonanza, and a sense of triumph that he had managed to accomplish this feat without caving into his fear of heights or of beestings, he eagerly clambered down to the cave entrance, scooped out a fingerful of honey from the wax, and slurped it up, reveling in its ambrosial sweetness. It had a faint flavor and aroma of jasmine— reminding him of the fragrance he had smelled in the moonlight on his first night at the cave. Chewing and sucking on the little wax chambers of the comb to extract all the honey he could, eventually he felt satiated.

He was careful to save the chewed wax from the honeycomb, storing it in one of his earthenware pots, realizing that he might find use for it, even once all the honey was gone. He had loved sculpting with beeswax as an art student, and loved the smell of burning beeswax votive tapers in the ancient churches of Spain and Italy on a memorable vacation he had taken in college during Summer break.

He managed to pick up the remaining honeycomb, and carefully brushed the dirt off the bottom of it from where it had landed, without losing much honey in doing so. He stashed what was left of the honeycomb with the wax he had already stored in one of the earthenware pots, and, licking the fragrant stickiness off his fingers as he went, he walked down to the stream to wash, feeling renewed by the entire sequence of events.

Something the guru (or Kala Cheetah) had said stuck in his mind, and now fed his rumination: "Things are not always what they seem to be". What an understatement! In the light of morphing figures, distinctly heard voices, the hallucinogenic transformation of his arms and hands into the furry limbs and claws of the panther, and his experience of roaring like a caged animal, not to mention the serendipitous appearance of a beehive dripping with honey right above the entrance to his cave, to conveniently feed his sudden sugar craving, his immediate response was, "No shit, Sherlock!"

things aren't always what they seem to be

"So now what?" he asked himself. "What am I supposed to *do* with all this?" assuming there must be some point or purpose to these experiences and revelations. Was this just a matter of shifting perceptions and perspectives on life, or did it perhaps indicate some sort of calling to re-channel his intentions, and focus his efforts in some new direction? After all, his supplies would run out soon, and he would presumably have to leave the cave and return to what he had formerly considered "the real world". To be sure, that definition now seemed almost laughable, having been superseded by events that currently seemed far more real than anything in his past experiences. But if he was to strike out in a new direction in his life, he had no idea where, or even how, or to what purpose, for that matter.

As he sat at the mouth of the cave, he felt his entire life pass before him, as if on parade. Scenes from every period of his life appeared like floats in the Rose Bowl Parade, the characters in each float being earlier versions of himself, waving to him as they went by, one by one, disappearing in the distance. The retrospective was quite surreal, and he couldn't help but wonder if there

things aren't always what they seem to be

was some specific meaning he was supposed to recognize or experience in all this.

It dawned on him that what he had been experiencing was oddly similar to what Plato described in his allegory of the cave, in his famous dialogue, The Republic. The life events appearing like floats in a parade were like the shadows cast on the wall of the cave, which the captives mistook for reality. But in his case, it was not the sunlight that allowed him to see clearly— it was the inner process he had been undergoing through the guidance of the guru, and the shift in perception that process elicited.

Socrates' objective in Plato's Republic was to open the eyes and minds of his disciples to truly understand the nature of reality, and the vital importance of learning, in order that the idea of the Good could prevail in real life. Moreover, he was intent on helping his disciples discover for themselves the process and means by which learning takes place— what Socrates described as "the craft", as opposed to the art, of learning. Socrates maintained that "It would not be an art that gives the soul vision, but a craft at labor under the assumption that the soul has its own innate

things aren't always what they seem to be

vision, but does not apply it properly. There must be some means for bringing this about."

Was the discovery and practice of the craft of learning perhaps the new direction he was to follow, the real purpose of his life? When he thought about it, he realized that both Kala Cheetah and his Guru had been modeling the craft of learning, showing him how to go about facing and conquering his fears by taming his mind, controlling his breath, and taking the help of focusing on a mantra. The *japa mala* was like the halter leading the young colt his father had talked about, keeping his mind heading in the right direction. The focus on the rock was like a metaphor for the inner process— cracking open the rough exterior of his turbulent mind to reveal the dazzling, beautiful, crystalline content within him. And his unexpected affection for the panther revealed to him an unsuspected capacity to feel empathy and an innate harmony with nature, even in its potentially terrifying manifestations.

Still, he remained with a sense there was something more to uncover in the dynamic of his fears. He began to ponder what specific things or situations tended to provoke the most fear for him.

things aren't always what they seem to be

What were his particular triggers? Could he use his newly discovered tools to neutralize them? Could he learn to take the firing pins out and disarm those habitual responses?

He realized that one of the consequences of his meditations on the rock and his correspondingly increased mental clarity was that he had, in effect, become a better listener, more willing to hear the answers to his own self-inquiry, even if uncomfortable. Having experienced being the unaffected witness of his thoughts, rather than their unwitting victim or captive, the possibility of a negative response to his self-questioning no longer felt threatening.

Other than sharks, spiders, and bats, there weren't a lot of creatures he was truly afraid of. His primary fears were more psychological and emotional. Fear of false accusations, fear of judgement, disapproval, and rejection, or abandonment, fear of inadequacy, fear of being misunderstood, fear of failure, fear of being unloved— all jostled for primacy in his attention. Though he suspected they were all somehow interconnected, he decided he'd try to look at each one, one at a time, to try to discern their source.

things aren't always what they seem to be

Reminded of *lectio divina*, St. Benedict's contemplative, "free association" approach to reading scripture, he decided to let each issue speak to him, and be willing to hear whatever it seemed to say without judgment, until nothing more seemed to come up, before moving on to the next one. He was instinctively aware, however, that a momentary silence did not necessarily mean the issue had been fully dealt with. Experience had already proven to be multi-layered, like an onion, and often you had to peel off many layers, one by one, to get to the sweetest and most flavorful ones.

Fear of false accusations seemed to be clamoring the loudest for his attention. Being falsely accused of something was not an isolated experience in his life. Even the mere suspicion of wrongdoing, though erroneous, had threatened or ruined relationships. It had happened many times. His earliest memory of it was as a small boy. He didn't even remember what the occasion was that triggered it, but he and his brother had been called on the carpet by his father, who had been persuaded by his older son that the younger had done something wrong, even though he hadn't. His father was convinced he was guilty, and failing to believe him was deeply wounding. He had always admired his father, who as a journalist was always pursuing the truth. That he failed to recognize the truth in his son's self-defense, was disillusioning to the extreme, and undermined his trust in his father, and subsequently, in anyone who claimed to care about the truth, but failed to recognize it.

Paternal disapproval was a far more painful punishment than any spanking or deprivation could be. His father's very WASPy way of looking stern, and saying in a sad, low, and chillingly cold voice, laden with negative judgment, "I'm *very* disappointed in you" was devastating. He and his brother had always been eager to receive their father's approval.

The collateral damage of this incident was the resentment he then felt toward his brother, who had convinced their father of his crime. He had always felt close, and looked up to his brother, but this accusation stung deeply. It did not even occur to him that his brother's accusation could have been based on a misperception, rather than on his desire to win their competition for parental approval, because (in his perception at least) his

things aren't always what they seem to be

little brother was their father's favorite. Whatever the "truth" of that unfortunate event, it left a mark on him that was compounded by every subsequent experience of being falsely accused of anything. Others' disbelief made him feel betrayed and insecure, misunderstood, and a failure. Only now did he start to realize that other's opinions of him were no more than their opinions, not absolute truths, and he could choose not to be affected by them.

Though he had also experienced false accusations in the workplace, and the political maelstrom they could generate, the arena in which they were most troublesome and emotionally hurtful had always been in his personal relationships: the need for some of the people closest to him to place blame on others for their own mistakes, misperceptions, or unhappiness resulted in him feeling at times like a movie screen for their projections. His past experience had often been one of knee-jerk defensiveness, which only tended to fuel others' conviction that he was, in fact, to blame. Shakespeare had pegged that dynamic when he said, "Methinks she doth protest too much", revealing the undeniable guilt of Lady Macbeth, and the human nature of trying to escape

things aren't always what they seem to be

responsibility and punishment for wrongdoing by dissembling and counter-blame.

Now, with his newfound experience of witness consciousness and self-inquiry, a new dynamic emerged for dealing with injustice and the evasive emotional dishonesty that sidestepped the underlying cause of his fear, and prevented its cure. It occurred to him that instead of asking himself, "*What* are you afraid of?" it might be better to ask, "*Who* is it that is afraid?" Even if others did project their own opinions and attitudes on him, his new insights let him see that a movie screen is unaffected by the images projected onto it, and so could he be. What seemed to determine his experience was the degree to which he identified with the accusations against him, or with the fear of what it would mean to his self-esteem if they were, in fact, proven justifiable. He was starting to see that, as the Buddhists love to say, "all is impermanence", and even if he had been guilty of some heinous act or abhorrent behavior in the past, there was a fundamental difference between *who* he was, and what he'd done. Who he was, essentially, was unchanging and eternal Consciousness, whereas *how* he was was in a constant state of flux. Others' belief in

things aren't always what they seem to be

accusations made against him did not make them true or permanent. So why identify with or become attached to something so ephemeral? See it, accept it without negative judgment, let it go—and learn from it! Though it seemed some actions and behaviors were more deeply rooted and left a more lasting mark on his sense of self than others, none, in fact, were permanent or definitive.

It dawned on him that here too, his guru and Kala Cheetah were modeling a new experience of self-perception, to help him see that his habitual answer to "Who am I?" was based on a fundamental misperception. If neither his guru nor Kala Cheetah were limited to a particular form, and both were, in fact, an expression of his own inner and fundamental self, then he needed to reassess his experiences of hurt and betrayal, and all the other things that provoked in him an experience of fear, or threatened his sense of wellbeing. He realized that he had a life-long pattern of struggling between self-doubt and arrogant over-confidence, and it now seemed that both polarities were based on a fundamental misunderstanding of who he really was, and a mistaken belief in his own doership. Both were driven by a misperception that he was lacking

things aren't always what they seem to be

some essential quality or ability, and a failure to recognize that Consciousness itself, not his limited ego identity, is the doer of all actions. By identifying with either some positive attribute or lack thereof, he discovered he was limiting himself to what he did or didn't do, and thereby denying his oneness with the irreducible Consciousness that made both his existence and his actions possible in the first place!

He was suddenly struck with the absurdity of identifying himself with any lack. For, if he was a manifestation of the same Consciousness he experienced in Baba, or even Kala Cheetah, how could that omnipresent and Supreme and Infinite Consciousness be diminished, or suffer insult, loss, humiliation, or betrayal? He, in fact, lacked nothing. He flashed on the verse in the Book of Genesis that asserts "God created humankind in God' own image and likeness, male and female.... And saw that it was good." The ancients clearly taught that we are participants in divinity, yet we overlook that simple statement as if it had no relationship to our experience of self-limitation!

Fear of disapproval, rejection, inadequacy, of being misunderstood, fear of failure, fear of

things aren't always what they seem to be

being unloved— now struck him as a sort of cosmic joke. Who was experiencing those states? God's own infinite being was manifesting in countless ever-changing forms, while pretending to identify and limit itself to those forms, only to discover that they were in fact limitless, and essentially illusory! It was like finally seeing that all matter is really nothing but energy in perpetual motion. It was his habitual tendency to avoid the discomfort of misidentification with both the accuser and the accusation that had plagued him throughout life. Was that evasive habit necessarily just his limited ego's deliberate avoidance of the truth of his experience, and therefore indicative of guilt, or was it perhaps not a sort of automatic, if involuntary, natural course correction in the ongoing journey of his life, underscoring his true and infinite nature?

As if to emphasize and confirm the implications of this insight, he heard in the distance the roar of the panther.

As he pondered the interconnectedness and the impermanence of all his fears and all his aspirations, he realized it was time for him to leave his cave, both metaphorically and literally.

things aren't always what they seem to be

Uncertain as to where this would lead him, he was at least clear that he shouldn't and couldn't just hide out in his cave with its bats and bugs and bees. He knew he needed to apply the lessons of his retreat to the challenge of everyday living, wherever that ended up being.

He carefully packed up his belongings, and the few meager supplies he had left, including the ball of beeswax from which he had now thoroughly extracted all its honey. He thought perhaps he'd create some little sculpture from it to commemorate his experience there. As he picked up his backpack and prepared to leave, he did experience a moment of wistful attachment and reluctance, for his retreat had been far more rewarding than he had ever imagined, and he couldn't help but feel a surge of gratitude for the place in which those formative experiences had occurred to him. But he knew he carried that experience within him, and it could not be confined to that particular cave, on that particular mountain, in that particular jungle. Just in case, however, de did manage to pry loose a large amethyst crystal from the geode at the cave entrance, as a sort of good luck memento of his adventure in self-discovery there.

things aren't always what they seem to be

Climbing down the mountain proved more arduous and slower going than he had anticipated. The terrain was rocky and rough, and the vegetation dense. It was also teeming with a wide variety of insects and other creatures, including snakes— pythons, cobras, and the short-tempered and deadly kraits the locals called the *pancha-pali*, or five-stepper— allegedly describing how far you'd get after the misfortune of being bitten by one. Fortunately, the monsoon had not yet arrived, so the snakes had not been flooded out of their underground dens by the rains, but caution was still advisable when trekking through the jungle undergrowth.

things aren't always what they seem to be

As he crossed the river at a shallow falls, he could see in the distance a cluster of shikaras— the dome-like towers— of several Hindu temples rising above the jungle greenery, and the ripening rice paddies beyond. Following along the course of the river, as he approached the temple complex and its surrounding village, he spotted a group of people bathing in the river, and detected a whiff of sulphur, and wisps of steam arising from the surface of a pool. "Wow! Hot springs!" he thought to himself. The mountain of his retreat turned out

things aren't always what they seem to be

to have been a dead volcano, and volcanic activity would clearly account for the hot springs. It struck him as oddly appropriate that his first contact with humans after his retreat would be in a setting dedicated to healing and blessing.

He started to remember stories about this place his guru used tell, long before he ever ventured up the mountain for his retreat. As if gradually recovering from amnesia, he recalled that legend had it that for centuries, yogis and sages used to gather here by the springs, and many, in fact, had lived in the caves of the mountain from which he had just descended. He flashed on Kala Cheetah's abrupt departure that day early on during his retreat, and wondered whether, rather than protectively sensing villagers hunting the shape-shifting leopard, he had, in fact,

things aren't always what they seem to be

run off to communicate with other sages hidden in the caves that riddled the mountain.

It was very odd that he had no memory of exactly how he had arrived at the cave in the first place, or even how he knew which of the mountain caves he had been assigned to for his retreat. It was as if his entire sense of present purpose and personal experience began the moment he arrived there at the cave, and nothing prior to that even mattered.

Some of the Adivasi villagers stared at him as he walked by. They seemed curious as to who this *pandu*— this white guy— might be, since most pilgrims, especially foreigners, came into town from the opposite side and the main access road, not the trail that led into the jungle. He walked past those who were bathing ritually in the hot springs of the river, past a more private spa, and onward to an ancient Shiva temple. Small, and with a low dome, it was not architecturally all that impressive, but it was clearly ancient and exuded that special vibration he had often recognized in places where prayer had been offered for millennia. He entered and sat down along the wall, watching the Brahmin priests perform the

things aren't always what they seem to be

bathing of the shivalingam— the central object of worship— and felt enveloped by the resonance of the Vedic mantras they chanted as they performed their rituals.

As he sat there, feeling that the place was strangely familiar, he began to ponder the insights that had come to him during his time in the cave— especially the sense of being called to a change of direction in life and a desire to help himself and others learn. This was not the first time he'd had the sense of being somewhere he had been before and forgotten, but with a new understanding of what that might mean both for now, and for the future.

things aren't always what they seem to be

He realized that, rather than identifying with a particular aspect of his life, or a particular skill set, or place he had lived, he had been, in fact, immersed in an ongoing process of reinventing himself. Yet none of the changes he underwent outwardly ever changed his essential nature. The illusion of reinventing himself was just an adaptive behavior. It allowed him to adjust to ever-changing circumstances and expand his awareness and understanding of both the process and fruit of his own being. He could already identify several things that he had at one point or another considered his "career", and yet none of them were permanent, nor adequately "defined" him. They were activities in which he had engaged for a time, as necessity, opportunity, or inclination dictated, whose impact on him he was just beginning to appreciate, and whose impact on others he scarcely imagined.

He was flooded with long-forgotten memories of going to the nearby riverbank to dig clay for the mold of a statue he had done of his guru's guru. Some South Indian shilpa shastris from Tirupati Temple were in the ashram creating a silver mandapam, or baldacchino, for the large murti of Baba's guru in the main temple. One of

things aren't always what they seem to be

them, named Umapati, had promised to teach him the entire casting process. The lost wax bronze casting technique had not changed in 5000 years.

After digging clay from the riverbank and dissolving it into a slurry in a bucket of water, and then passing the sludge through a sieve to remove pebbles and large grains of sand or pieces of roots— the mix was then applied to the figure he had made from beeswax gathered from a huge hive under the ashram eaves. The mud was allowed to air dry, and then placed on a bed of coals. The coal used was high density bitumen coal, not simple wood charcoal. The most sophisticated piece of even remotely "modern" equipment in the whole process was a bellows with a hand crank like a bicycle pedal. Pointing it at the coals and cranking until the coals turned bright red resulted in the wax in the mold burning up completely. Removed with a pair of steel tongs like his grandparents had by their fireplace, the mold was allowed to cool down.

Umapati calculated how much metal would be needed to fill the mold by filling it with water and pouring that water into a measuring cup to assess the volume. Umapati told him that the

things aren't always what they seem to be

murti should be cast in an alloy of five metals— gold, silver, copper, zinc, and iron— the *pancha loha* used for sacred images. Estimating the weight of each metal and its proportions to the overall mix, he remembered taking the State Transport bus into Mumbai and acquiring the base metals from a scrap metal dealer. The gold and silver he used were bits of broken jewelry and the wire he had used to string malas for fellow devotees. Loading the components into a crucible, with the same tongs, Umapati placed the crucible back on the bed of coals and told him to keep cranking the bellows until all five metals had melted. He stirred the mix occasionally to make sure the metals were evenly distributed and well mixed. The foam of impurities rose to the surface, which he skimmed off with a deft flick of a metal bar at his side, and then when the dross had burned off, he carefully lifted the crucible and tipped its contents into the inverted mold, which sat packed in a bed of sand to prevent cracking and spillage. Once the molten metal had cooled to the touch, he gave his American apprentice a handful of small steel chisels he had made for him— and showed him how to gently chip off the baked mud of the mold, revealing the metal figure inside. Finally using fine

things aren't always what they seem to be

chisels, a rasp, and some emery paper to remove irregularities and polish the highlights, the figure was complete. Reheating it, after removing it from the coals and brushing it off, it was painted with a sort of india ink as a patina, and then buffed with a coat of melted beeswax. Though hardly a good likeness of his guru's guru, the figure was brought to Baba for his blessing, and the shilpa shastri team treated it with utmost reverence.

He realized this sculptural process was, in fact, a metaphor for his own growth process—enduring the intense heat, burning off the emotional dross of his life, the scraping and shaping, the hammer blows and the polishing that hopefully would reveal a figure that expressed, however imperfectly, some inner beauty worth sharing. He wondered if the same could be said about any of his other various "careers". He had been a teacher, a writer, a singer, a gardener, a cook, and an interpreter. He realized none of his activities had been a waste of time, and all of them came into use in one way or another. Moreover, it even struck him that each had made him better at the others.

things aren't always what they seem to be

"I wonder what's next?" he asked himself in a pensive mood, as he bowed to the Shivalinga. He held out his right palm to the pujari to receive the prasad— the blessed mixture with which the icon had been bathed, and thereby imbued with its presumed sanctity— and then he left the temple.

He walked on past the samadhi temple where his guru's guru was buried, and through the village, past the chai shops and flower vendors and the store selling all manner of religious figures, incense, fragrant attars, shawls, clothing, and other devotional items, to the main road. He was struck

things aren't always what they seem to be

by how much the village had prospered and grown over the years since his first visit.

As he continued down the road toward the main highway, he saw the dome of the temple of his guru's ashram rise above the greenery. As he read a sign by the front gate identifying the samadhi shrine, the burial site, of his guru, and the restrictions on when it could be visited, he was suddenly shaken, as if from a dream. His vivid experiences of his guru in the mountain cave were suddenly recast as either purely imaginary or hallucinogenic, as the guru had apparently "left his body" forty years ago! He was amazed to realize how fluid time was, and felt as if he was observing a series of flash-backs in a movie interwoven into his present experience of reality. It was a bit disorienting because though he now had vivid recall of the years he spent with his guru in the ashram, the intervening years since his guru took samadhi (as the devout describe the departure of a saint), were a sort of blank. He had no recollection of how he had ended up at the mountain cave, or how he had concluded he did so by his guru's command. Memory, he mused, is clearly an elusive, selective, and perhaps

things aren't always what they seem to be

unreliable thing. Yet it was also a guide, and sometimes even an inspiration.

The power of remembrance now struck him powerfully and gave a whole new meaning to the exhortation by Jesus to his disciples at the Last Supper, (and repeated to the faithful in every mass ever since—) "do this in remembrance of me". Moreover, it was not lost on him that the Greek word for remembrance used in the earliest Gospel texts was *anamnesis*, which implies not just a sort of passive recollection, but an active experience of *reliving* that experience as a present event. That reliving was now taking on a whole new meaning for him as he embraced the sense that time itself is an illusion, and his past, present, and future were integrally connected, and essentially both simultaneous and eternal.

Despite his love for his teacher, he decided against attempting to enter the ashram or the samadhi shrine, preferring to hold in his heart the memory of his experience there years ago memory of his experience there years ago.

things aren't always what they seem to be

when the master was still living. The thought that some new bureaucracy of ashram administration might prevent him from entering, was distressing. The certainty that the policies currently governing the ashram had passed into the hands of those who felt compelled to reshape the ashram's appearance and aesthetic to conform with the tastes of the current leader, rather than to preserve the eclectic original charm of his guru's reign, was even more so. He stood in devout remembrance before the ashram gateway, palms folded reverently, offered thanks for what had been, and moved on to the bus stop nearby to await the next State Transport bus to take him to the train station and from there, on to Mumbai. Time for a new chapter, he mused.

Though he noticed the road had been much improved since the days when he had lived

things aren't always what they seem to be

in the Ashram, the view from the bus remained largely unchanged. He remembered his first visit there he had noted that being in an airconditioned bus that sealed you off from the heat, the sounds, and smells of India was a bit like watching a National Geographic film— all very scenic and picturesque but failing to convey the full experiential reality.

Somehow the experience of the visuals was significantly more impactful when couched in the complex smells and sounds of the area. Like analyzing the formula of an expensive perfume, he sniffed air to see how many and what distinct smells he could identify. The were floral fragrances— frangipani, champa, mogra, and roses; there were culinary fragrances— oil, ghee, cumin, cardamom, ginger, chillies and countless other spices, fruits and vegetables— then there were animal fragrances— buffalo and cow dung, human feces too, and sweat. This mélange set a distinct stamp on each village and farm as he rattled past them on his State Transport bus toward Mumbai and his uncertain future.

Adivasi villages still dotted the entire landscape, interspersed with rice paddies and

things aren't always what they seem to be

banana plantations, and groves of coconut palms, cashews and mango trees. As they got nearer the city, the villages took on a more substantial appearance. The thatched roofs and mud and wattle construction of the houses gave way increasingly to cinder-block walls and corrugated tin roofs— construed as "modern" by the local tribespeople. Electricity had clearly arrived everywhere, as the garish lights of colored bulbs and neon signs, and the strident blare of Indian pop music on the radio clearly revealed. Such, to the rural poor, were clear signs of their upward mobility and success. Even the smells had become a bit more "industrial".

As he mused on the relativity of notions of success, he found himself reflecting on his own past— or at least what he could currently remember of it. He had sometimes felt unsuccessful, since even the things he most loved to do never seemed to earn him a living, and sometimes for that very reason he had felt obligated to change direction and try something else.

He now started to realize that "earning a living" was a social construct that was not, in fact,

things aren't always what they seem to be

the source of survival or wellbeing, but merely the reason and apparent means society ascribed to what it construed as necessary. And that necessity was whatever local custom and popular opinion assumed would assure the minimal level of comfort and respectability required, in order to be deemed a "successful" human being and member of the community!

He realized gratefully that however anyone else might judge his level of success, he had never gone homeless, or hungry, or involuntarily naked. He flashed on his timely discovery of the beehive at the cave, despite his cocky presumption that trusting in divine Providence was foolish and naïve. It made him recognize that though it had felt like circumstances had forced him to change directions and repeatedly have to find or create some sort of new "professional identity", to "reinvent himself", in truth, only his doing had changed, not his being. Thinking he had had to reinvent himself in the past had actually led him to feel like an imposter. Sometimes it felt like he had to hide his past. At others, he felt he had to overstate his present or presume too much about his potential future. The result of both was a sort of insecurity and self-doubt that he felt he had to

things aren't always what they seem to be

conceal from others, lest he be exposed as a fraud. He remembered his guru saying, "The Self never dies", and logically, he concluded, it can therefore never be reinvented— it can only express itself in an infinite variety of ways.

With the advent of the internet and social media, self-promotion became surprisingly easy to do without immediately appearing to be insufferably egocentric or deliberately deceitful. The danger was that objective fact could be easily confused with subjective reality, and the risk of potential damage to both the narrator and the public, due to that potential confusion, was not insignificant. The more open he became, the more adaptable he was, the less attached he was to any particular manifestation, and the more he began to understand the implications of the oneness he had experienced with both his guru and Kala Cheetah. That oneness implicitly extended to all creatures and all existence. He could only feel like a fraud if he chose to identify with his limitation, and could only be fulfilled by identifying with and fully embracing his essentially infinite nature.

As he began to embrace that awareness, he realized that the very act of self-identification with

things aren't always what they seem to be

any specific, limited form was, inevitably, if unintentionally, fraudulent, or at least misleading. The identities we choose are like the clothes we wear— repeatedly subject to costume changes. And like actors, we may have roles or costumes we particularly enjoy, but they will ever be separate from the actor. How we manifest, the actions we perform, and how we experience them do not adequately define us or fully express the reality of our infinite nature.

Consequently, he saw that it was presumptuous and silly to even think that we could be or need to be "reinvented". The activities we abandon or new activities we adopt, whatever they may be, could possibly change our appearance to others, and even our experience of the moment, but cannot change our true nature. The key to fulfillment, it seemed, lay only in how we choose to express it. It was simply a matter of being, not of doing. Being, he now realized, is the source not only of all experience, but also of ultimate fulfillment. Life was the ongoing learning process of fully being. What a great adventure!

As the State Transport Bus rattled on toward the train that would take him to Mumbai, the

things aren't always what they seem to be

visible environment in which he found himself transitioned from looking out at the jungle from a cave in a mountain, to a tiny village lost in a time warp of thatched huts, water buffalos and rice paddies, and then on to an increasingly populated, noisy and chaotic reality of South Asian urban life.

Vivid colors flashed by. He saw the local flora echoed in the dazzling pattern of Indian textiles, from homespun cotton to exquisite silks and gold trimmed brocades befitting royalty. Combinations of colors that had at first seemed garish and tacky compared to the subtler pastel palette of his New England upbringing, now made total sense as nature's exuberant local self-expression. The smells too seemed to compete for dominance between the rancid stench of exhaust fumes, feces, urine and gutter effluvia, the intoxicating aromas of rare attars and sublime incense, exotic flowers, tropical fruits, and the delectable smells of spices and street food. This sensory cornucopia, it struck him, was a perfect encapsulation of our multidimensional reality. Suddenly all thought of what he should now "do" with his life and his future was reduced to simply "embrace and enjoy it!" No other teacher or school was necessary, and the only future is now.

things aren't always what they seem to be

things aren't always what they seem to be

About the Author

Robert H. Stucky is a multi-lingual writer, speaker and teacher who draws on his global life experience to share insights into our collective search for meaning and fulfillment. Widely travelled, he has been an artist, interpreter, spiritual director, and retreat leader on five continents. He encourages critical thinking and spiritual open-mindedness as keys to living fully.

Made in the USA
Middletown, DE
19 October 2024